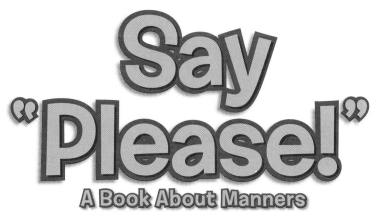

Say "Please!"

A Book About Manners

adapted by Catherine Lukas

based on the original teleplay by Janice Burgess

illustrated by Zina Saunders

SIMON SPOTLIGHT/NICK JR.

New York   London   Toronto   Sydney

visit us at www.abdopublishing.com

Reinforced library bound edition published in 2007 by Spotlight, a division of ABDO Publishing Group, Edina, Minnesota. Published by agreement with Simon Spotlight, Simon & Schuster Children's Publishing Division.

Text by Catherine Lukas based on the original teleplay by Janice Burgess. Illustrations by Zina Saunders. Based on the TV series *Nick Jr. The Backyardigans*™ as seen on Nick Jr.® Reprinted with permission of Simon Spotlight, Simon & Schuster Children's Publishing Division. All rights reserved.

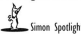 Simon Spotlight

An Imprint of Simon & Schuster Children's Publishing Division
1230 Avenue of the Americas, New York, New York 10020

Library of Congress Cataloging-In-Publication Data

This title was previously cataloged with the following information:
Lukas, Catherine
   Say "Please" / by Catherine Lukas ; illustrated by Zina Saunders
     p. cm. (The Backyardigans ; bk. #5)
   ISBN 978-1-4169-1386-3 (paperback)
   I. Saunders, Zina, ill. II. Title. III. Series.

   [E]--dc22

ISBN-13: 978-1-59961-160-0 (reinforced library bound edition)
ISBN-10: 1-59961-160-0 (reinforced library bound edition)

All Spotlight books are reinforced library binding and
manufactured in the United States of America.

"It is I, Princess CleoTasha of ancient Egypt," said Tasha. "It's great to have a big palace and servants who wait on me. Hey! Where *are* my servants, anyway?"

Princess CleoTasha clapped her hands. "Servant Tyrone! Servant Pablo! Servant Austin! Time to wait on me!"

The three loyal royal servants hurried over to her. "I'm thirsty," she said. "Bring me a glass of water!"

"But there is no water, O Princess," said Pablo. "The Nile River has dried up."

"Well, fill it back up!" said the princess.

"Only you can, O Princess," said Austin. "You must ask Sphinx Uniqua to tell you the secret of the Nile. Only then will the water return."

"But first you must bring her three presents. They are hidden all over Egypt," said Tyrone.

"And we'll help you find them," said Austin.

Princess CleoTasha and her loyal royal servants set off to find the presents.

"There's just one thing about Princess CleoTasha," said Pablo.

"She never says 'please,'" whispered Tyrone.

"Or 'thank you,'" mumbled Austin.

"What's the first present for the sphinx, Servant Tyrone?" asked Princess CleoTasha.

"It's called the Jewel of the Waters," answered Tyrone. "It is found inside the Hidden Pyramid."

They walked and walked and finally stopped in the Valley of the Pyramids. Then they noticed Servant Tyrone was leaning against something . . . something that they couldn't even see! It was the Hidden Pyramid! *Swish!* A door opened up.

Princess CleoTasha made Servant Tyrone go in first.
"Here it is, Princess," he said, pointing to a gleaming jewel.

"I found it!" the princess yelled, grabbing the huge jewel.
"The first present for the sphinx." She handed it to Tyrone. "It's heavy.
You carry it," she ordered him.

"She never says 'please,'" he murmured to himself.

"Okay, what's the second present, Servant Pablo?" asked the princess.

"It's the yellow lotus flower that grows on the Cliffs of Karnak," said Pablo.

"Let's get going," she ordered. "And don't forget my stuff."

The three loyal royal servants sighed. Once again she had forgotten to say "please" and "thank you."

After a long journey, they arrived at the Cliffs of Karnak.

"How am I supposed to get all the way up there?" asked the princess.

"The stairs, O Princess," Pablo explained.

"You go first," she ordered.

Servant Pablo shook his head. Once again she had not asked nicely.

Up, up, up they climbed. At the top of the cliff was a beautiful meadow filled with colorful lotus flowers.

Suddenly Servant Pablo spotted the only yellow flower and pointed to it.

"Oh! The yellow lotus flower! I found it!" the princess cried. She plucked the flower and handed it to Pablo. "You carry it. I have to walk down all those stairs."

"So do I," Pablo said quietly as he followed her down the stairs.

"Behold, I found the second present for the sphinx!" announced the princess as she reached the bottom of the cliff. "Two presents down, one to go. Where to next?"

"To get the third present we must travel to the Secret Oasis," said Austin.

"Remind me, what's an oasis?" asked the princess.

"It's a green place with trees and water in the middle of the desert," Austin replied.

"Let's get that last present now," ordered the princess. "And don't forget my stuff."

The three loyal royal servants were all thinking the same thing: She forgot to say "please" again.

They all walked and walked until they reached the Secret Oasis.
"The third present is a drink of water from the Secret Oasis," said
Austin, handing the princess a golden cup.

"Great! I've got the third present!" the princess cheered. She scooped up the crystal-clear water and handed it to Servant Austin. "You carry it," she demanded. "Now that I have all three presents, it's time to go talk to that sphinx! Let's go, my loyal royal servants. To Sphinx Uniqua!"

They traveled through the desert along the dried-up banks of the Nile. At last they saw Sphinx Uniqua.

"Greetings, Sphinx Uniqua," said the princess. "I am the Royal Princess CleoTasha, and I have brought you three presents. They are the Jewel of the Waters, the yellow lotus flower, and a golden cup of water from the Secret Oasis."

"Thank you so much!" said Sphinx Uniqua. "What lovely presents! Did you get them all by yourself?"

"Of course not, O Sphinx," replied the princess. "My loyal royal servants helped me. And they carried all my stuff."

"I see. Did you say 'thank you' for all of their help?" Sphinx Uniqua asked.

"Well, no," said the princess. "But will you tell me the secret of the Nile so there will be water in Egypt again?"

"Okay," replied the sphinx.

"The secret to almost everything is to always say 'please' and 'thank you.' You can start by saying 'thank you' to your servants who did all the work for you," whispered Sphinx Uniqua to the princess.

The princess looked surprised. Then she turned to her servants.

"Thank you for helping me and for doing all of the work," she said nicely.

"You're welcome!" said all three of them together.

"And thank you, O Sphinx, for telling me the secret of the Nile," Princess CleoTasha said.

"You're welcome," said the Sphinx.

And just like that, the Nile River began filling back up with water.

Everyone cheered!

"And now won't you all *please* join me for a snack?" Tasha asked them politely.

"Thank you! We'd love to!" said everyone else.

And they all went back to Tasha's house for a snack.